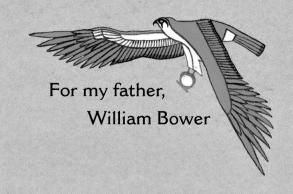

For my father,
William Bower

# TAMARA BOWER

# HOW THE AMAZON QUEEN FOUGHT THE PRINCE OF EGYPT

## ATHENEUM BOOKS FOR YOUNG READERS

New York   London   Toronto   Sydney

Long ago, in a place called Khor, there was a Land of Women near Assyria, where the Amazons lived. There the Amazon women lived free, without men. They rode horses and hunted and were happy at their will.

But one day scouts made a report to their Amazon queen, Serpot. An army of Egyptian soldiers and their Assyrian allies were approaching and making camp close by.

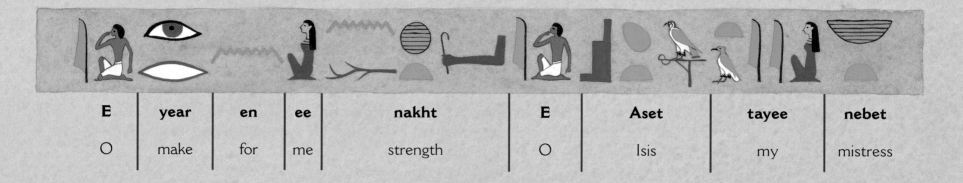

| E | year | en | ee | nakht | E | Aset | tayee | nebet |
|---|------|-----|-----|----------|---|------|-------|---------|
| O | make | for | me | strength | O | Isis | my | mistress |

Queen Serpot met with her Amazon leaders. She looked out at the small number of her troops and cried, "**Give me strength, O Isis, my mistress**, and Osiris, great god! The Egyptian army has made camp outside our fortress!"

Serpot thought of a plan. She called Ashteshyt, her youngest sister. "Dress as a man, as a soldier in the enemy's army, and go to their camp. Learn everything about their troops and the name of their leader. Go now and hurry."

So Ashteshyt went out, dressed as a man. She wore a false beard and the helmet and clothes of the enemy. Fierce guards armed with spears and knives stood at the entrance to the camp, but they let her pass, believing that she was one of their soldiers. Though her heart beat with fear, Ashteshyt walked about the camp as if she belonged there. No one noticed that she was a woman. She learned everything that was going on in the camp, without anyone recognizing her.

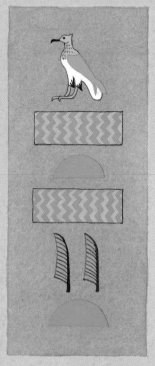

**ASHTESHYT**

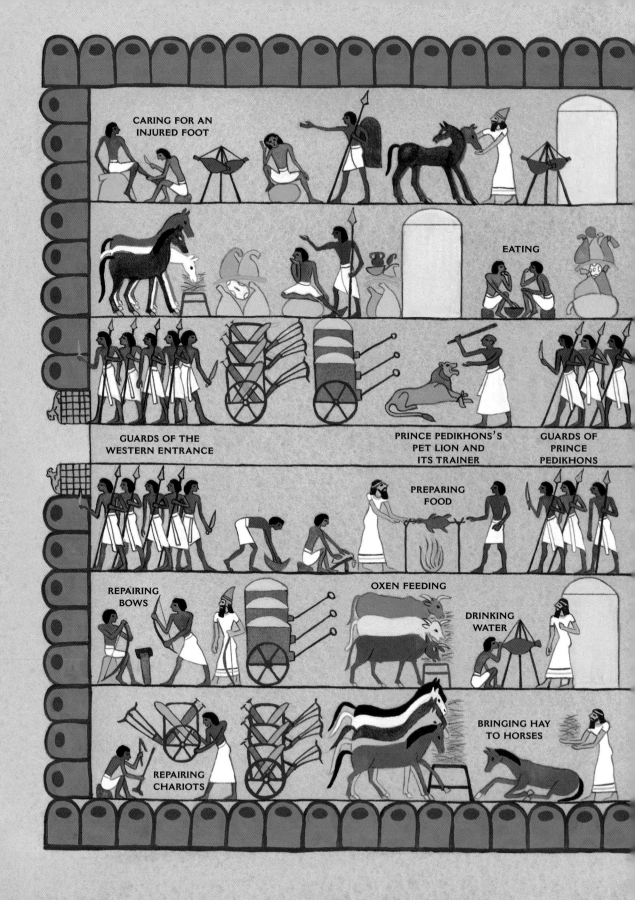

CARING FOR AN INJURED FOOT

EATING

GUARDS OF THE WESTERN ENTRANCE

PRINCE PEDIKHONS'S PET LION AND ITS TRAINER

GUARDS OF PRINCE PEDIKHONS

PREPARING FOOD

REPAIRING BOWS

OXEN FEEDING

DRINKING WATER

REPAIRING CHARIOTS

BRINGING HAY TO HORSES

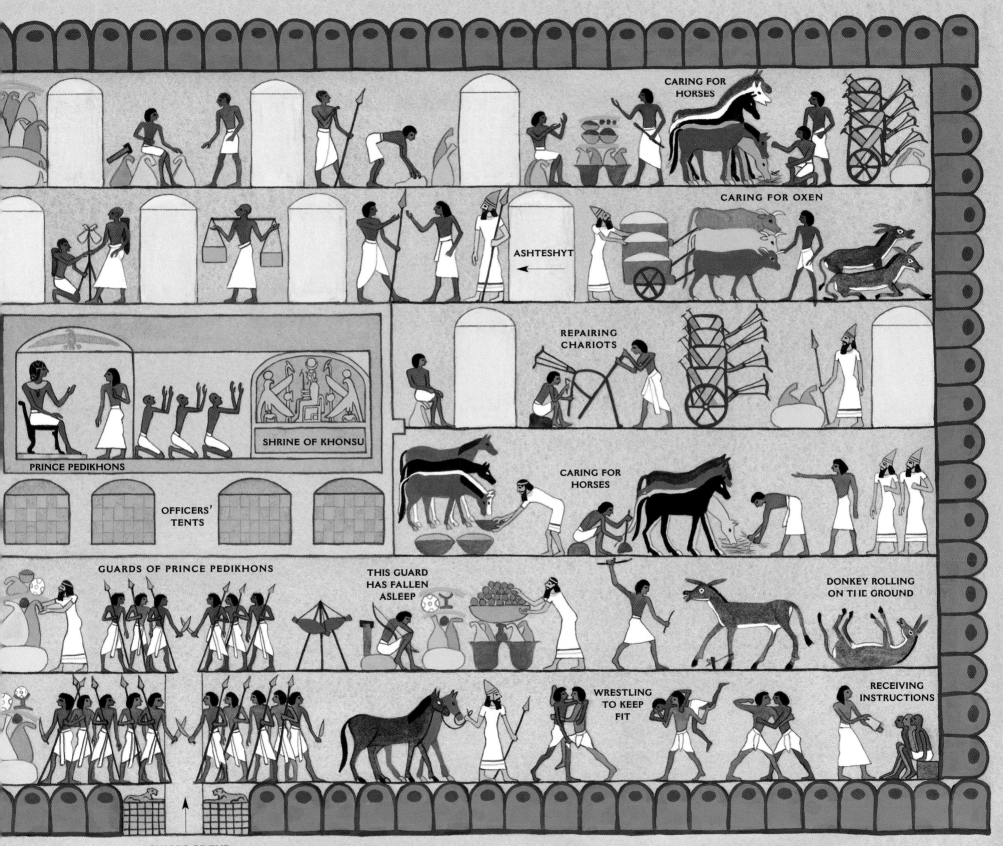

CARING FOR HORSES

CARING FOR OXEN

ASHTESHYT

REPAIRING CHARIOTS

CARING FOR HORSES

SHRINE OF KHONSU

PRINCE PEDIKHONS

OFFICERS' TENTS

GUARDS OF PRINCE PEDIKHONS

THIS GUARD HAS FALLEN ASLEEP

DONKEY ROLLING ON THE GROUND

WRESTLING TO KEEP FIT

RECEIVING INSTRUCTIONS

GUARDS OF THE SOUTHERN ENTRANCE

| imi | gereg | er | aha | er | wa | mesha | en | haset |
|------|-------------|------|----------|------|-----|-------|-----|------------------|
| make | preparations | for | fighting | for | an | army | of | the foreign land |

Ashteshyt returned to her sister Serpot. She told the queen everything she had seen. She described the camp in detail, and the enemy's leader, Prince Pedikhons.

Serpot said, "We have heard of this evil serpent of an Egyptian. He has fought against many chiefs. But we will defeat him. Let the trumpet and the horn sound in the Land of Women. And let it be said, brave women, **prepare for combat against a foreign army** that stands outside!"

Soon armies from all the regions of the Land of Women assembled at the fortress.

Queen Serpot inspected **the women equipped with their weapons** and their armor. She was pleased. She said to her soldiers, "Be strong and take courage! Isis, the great goddess, leads our army. Osiris, the great god, will bring us victory!"

| na | sehemut | netet | sedebehu | ema | nayu | ahau |
|----|---------|-------|----------|-----|------|------|
| the | women | who | were equipped | with | their | weapons |

Queen Serpot gave careful orders. The women warriors listened to her every word. They said, "Serpot, our queen, is with us. She will not abandon us!"

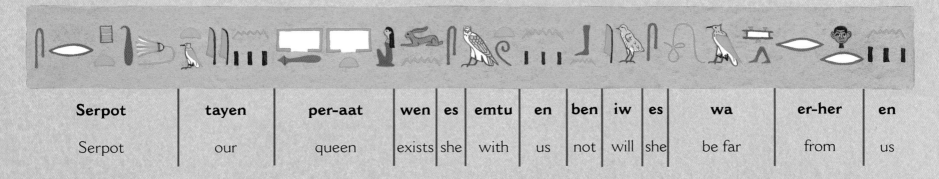

| Serpot | tayen | per-aat | wen | es | emtu | en | ben | iw | es | wa | er-her | en |
|--------|-------|---------|-----|-----|------|-----|-----|-----|-----|-----|--------|-----|
| Serpot | our | queen | exists | she | with | us | not | will | she | be far | from | us |

The Amazons went out to meet the Egyptian army. **They called out curses and taunts, the speech of warriors.**

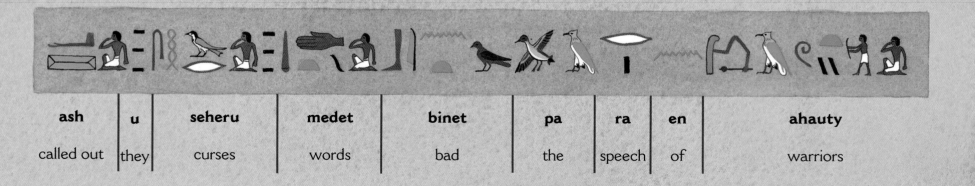

| ash | u | seheru | medet | binet | pa | ra | en | ahauty |
|---|---|---|---|---|---|---|---|---|
| called out | they | curses | words | bad | the | speech | of | warriors |

Serpot led her troops. She fought like a bird of prey, **like a raging leopard**. Each Amazon fought like ten men. The Egyptians dropped their weapons and fled.

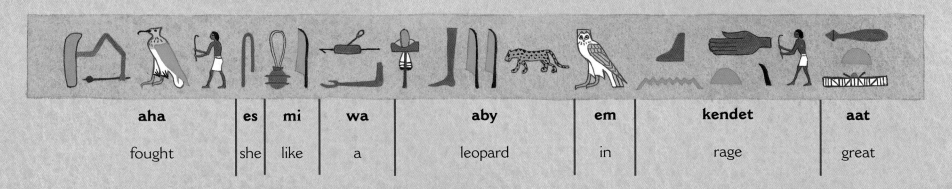

| aha | es | mi | wa | aby | em | kendet | aat |
|-----|-----|-----|-----|-----|-----|--------|-----|
| fought | she | like | a | leopard | in | rage | great |

Prince Pedikhons did not fight. He watched the battle from atop a hill. He gnashed his teeth and cried, "I won't stand for this! Women defeating my soldiers? No! Tomorrow this army of women will suffer a painful defeat. It will be beautiful after the bitterness of today!"

**PEDIKHONS**

| wenem | ef | mi | wa | per-a | seweri | ef | mi | wa | nakht-a |
|--------|------|-------|-----|-------|---------|------|-------|-----|----------|
| ate | he | like | a | hero | drank | he | like | a | strongman |

He went to his tent. **He drank and ate like a hero**. He thought about what he should do.

On the morning of the next day, Prince Pedikhons donned his armor and took up his weapons. He was like a roaring lion, like a bull bursting with strength.

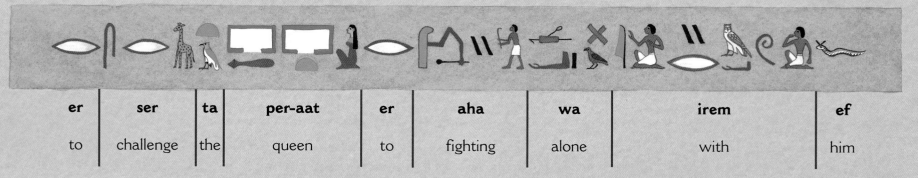

| er | ser | ta | per-aat | er | aha | wa | irem | ef |
|---|---|---|---|---|---|---|---|---|
| to | challenge | the | queen | to | fighting | alone | with | him |

He sent a messenger to the fortress, to Queen Serpot, **challenging the queen to single combat**. Serpot and her leaders listened in silence.

Ashteshyt said to her sister, "Yesterday you fought long and bravely. Now let me go to the battlefield to fight this vile Egyptian."

Serpot answered, "No, I am not a coward, nor do I tire easily. I will don my armor and fight this Egyptian scorpion."

So the queen's soldiers brought her armor and weapons to her. The Amazons opened the gates of the fortress, and Serpot went out, announcing combat to Prince Pedikhons. Each was ready to meet the other.

"Pedikhons, you worm!" Serpot cursed. "You will be to me as an insect in the mouth of a bird. I will smash your face into your neck. I will break your legs into your heels!"

"Serpot, you will flee from me as a gazelle from a lion!" Pedikhons swore. "Your limbs will weaken. Your knees will tremble!"

And so they fought. Their blows were beautiful, their strokes deceitful. **They rushed at each other like vultures.** They attacked like panthers. The ground trembled from their battle.

| as | | u | er | se | neb | mi | neriu |
|----|---|---|----|----|-----|----|-------|
| rushed | | they | at | man | each | like | vultures |

They made feints. They struck. They jumped. **Neither gave way to the other.** They fought all through the day.

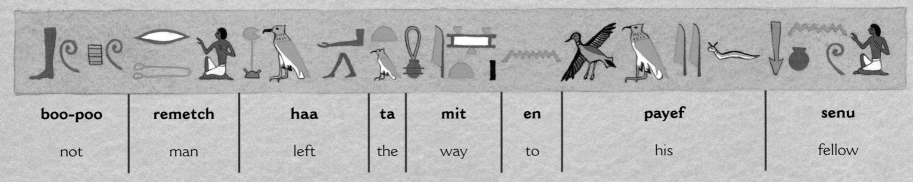

| boo-poo | remetch | haa | ta | mit | en | payef | senu |
|---------|---------|-----|-----|-----|-----|-------|------|
| not | man | left | the | way | to | his | fellow |

Queen Serpot said, "**You fighter of Egypt! The sun has set.** It will rise over us again tomorrow."

The prince agreed. "One does not fight in the dark."

They stood together.

The queen asked, "Tell me, Pedikhons, why have you come here to the Land of Women?"

Prince Pedikhons answered, "I heard stories of the Land of Women who fight. And I came here to see your Amazon warriors with my own eyes. I never believed woman could conquer man." He turned to her. "Now I am so moved by the courage and strength of you and your women warriors that I will put down my sword and stand by your side."

| I | ahauty | en | Ta-Meri | pa | ra | wah | ef |
|---|--------|-----|---------|------|-----|---------|-----|
| O | fighter | of | Egypt | the | sun | has set | it |

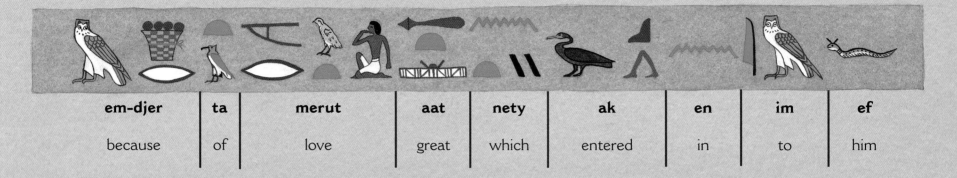

| em-djer | ta | merut | aat | nety | ak | en | im | ef |
|---------|-----|-------|-------|------|---------|-----|-----|-----|
| because | of | love | great | which | entered | in | to | him |

It was then that Prince Pedikhons looked at Queen Serpot and saw that she was his equal. And he did not know where on Earth he was, **from the great love that entered into him.**

And it was then that Queen Serpot looked at the prince and saw that he was her equal. And she did not know where on Earth she was, from the great love that entered into her.

And later Serpot and Pedikhons made an alliance and conquered India together.

# A NOTE ABOUT THIS STORY

Our story is an episode in a longer story called "Egyptians and Amazons," a tale that belongs to a group of stories known as the *Story-Cycle of King Petubast*. The papyrus scroll of "Egyptians and Amazons" is now in the Kunsthistorisches Museum in Vienna, Austria. This papyrus is in tatters, with less than half of the story preserved and without the beginning. I have stayed close to what we have of the original story, only rewording it and adding small details. The ancient scroll starts with Prince Pedikhons leaving the entourage of King Petubast and arriving in the land of Khor. Khor is an ancient name for Syria, and in this case, it also refers to Assyria. According to our story, a region within Khor is ruled by Amazons under the rule of Queen Serpot. Pedikhons heads an army of Egyptian and Assyrian soldiers.

The stories in the *Story-Cycle of King Petubast* may have been written in response to inquiries made by King Ptolemy II about Egyptian history. Since few women could read and write in ancient Egypt, these stories were likely to have been written by men. While these stories have much fantasy and romance, they do concern some real historical figures. Prince Pedikhons was the son of Prince Inaros of Heliopolis and a kinsman of King Petubast. Though the stories were written during the Greco-Roman period, they are about rulers from an earlier time known as the Third Intermediate Period, when Egypt was ruled by many petty princes

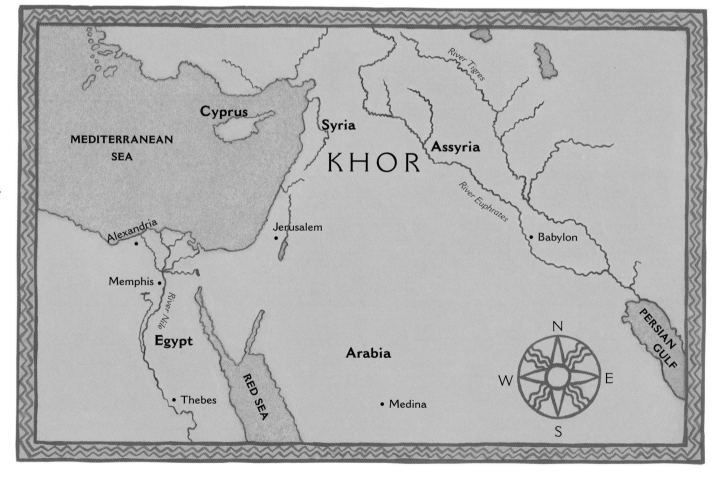

who fought one another for power and prestige. Petubast II was king of Tanis, a town in the Nile Delta, in the north of Egypt.

Amazons were described by the ancient Greeks as tribes of fierce women warriors who lived together without men. They rejected the traditional roles of wives, instead learning to ride horses, to hunt, and to wage war. Amazons have been dismissed as myth, but there is growing evidence that societies with warrior women existed in the ancient Near East and in other parts of the world. Archaeologists have discovered graves of women buried with weapons and armor in Ukraine and other areas. But so far, there is no concrete evidence of female tribes that excluded men.

Our story is clearly inspired by Greek myths and may derive from the story of Achilles, who fought against the Amazon queen Penthesilea when she came to defend Troy in the Trojan War. Achilles killed the queen, but fell in love with her as she lay dying. There are no Egyptian stories of Amazon tribes before Egypt made contact with Greece. The Egyptians did have war goddesses, such as Neith, a creator goddess whose symbol is a shield with crossed arrows, and the lion-headed Sakhmet; and they also worshipped Astarte and Anat, warrior goddesses from Syria.

The goddess Isis and her husband, Osiris, were important deities in Egyptian religion. They were said to be the first rulers of Egypt and taught the people to grow crops. Osiris was killed by his evil brother but was revived by Isis, and he became god of the underworld. Isis was especially known for her magical powers. The cult of Osiris and Isis was especially popular during the Greco-Roman period, and it spread from Egypt throughout the Roman Empire.

Pedikhons means "gift of Khonsu." Khonsu, a moon god, was the son of the god Amun and the goddess Mut; he was worshipped at Thebes and became a god of healing and of war. Serpot's name means "lotus." "Ashteshyt" is a non-Egyptian word whose meaning we don't know.

# ABOUT HIEROGLYPHS

Ancient Egyptian hieroglyphs are one of the most beautiful writing systems in the world. Hieroglyphs are made up of pictures of people, animals, plants, and objects.

Hieroglyphs can be written in either direction—horizontally from left to right or right to left, or vertically from top to bottom. Individual signs are always turned so that they look toward the beginning of the inscription. The hieroglyphs in this book are written left to right, so the signs face toward the left.

Hieroglyphs are not a simple alphabet, nor are they "picture writing" in the sense that the pictures always symbolize an idea. Some hieroglyphs represent an idea, and some represent sounds; many may represent a sound in one context or an idea in another. Usually the words are spelled out first in sounds, and then at the end of the word is an image for its meaning, called a "determinative." Sometimes the determinative has a single stroke under or next to it to show that it represents meaning rather than sound.

Because many words were spelled the same, the determinative was important for understanding the meaning. A determinative could have several possible meanings, depending upon the spelling of the word that it followed.

There are no vowels written in hieroglyphs. Because of this, we don't know for sure how ancient Egyptian was pronounced. The pronunciations are our guesses at what they sounded like.

Though we are using hieroglyphs in this book, our story was originally written in demotic. Demotic was an ancient Egyptian cursive script that evolved from the earlier cursive hieratic. It uses a grammar and vocabulary that make it distinct from the earlier Egyptian and was probably derived from the type of Egyptian spoken in the Delta, in the north of Egypt. It first appeared in 600 B.C.E. and eventually replaced hieratic. Demotic is one of the three types of writing on the famous Rosetta stone.

Demotic is *always* written from right to left, while hieroglyphs may be written from either direction. Here is an example of demotic and its hieroglyphic equivalent (to be read backward):

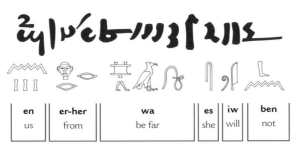

It is difficult to make a literal word-for-word translation of the language of ancient Egyptians, as their sentence structure was different from ours, and also because they used different expressions. In this book, we have translated the hieroglyphs word for word underneath, but also have highlighted the translated sentence, as we would say it, within the story's text.

# EXPLANATION OF SYMBOLS

The paintings in this book are based on both ancient Egyptian and ancient Assyrian art. Because we have no pictures of Amazons from Assyria or Egypt, some artistic license has been taken.

Both Egyptian and Assyrian art were often meant to be read symbolically. Assyrian artists often looked at Egyptian art and made their own interpretations of the same symbolic images. The following list is a guide to some of the symbols and meanings contained in some of the paintings.

**Page 6:** The oval on the upper left corner is a sign for the name of a country, and the hieroglyphs read, "The Land of Women." The Amazon fortress is based on an Assyrian design.

**Page 7:** The oval country sign here reads, "Khor."

**Page 9:** Serpot's feather crown and her hairstyle are based on a carving of the goddess Astarte. Her throne and the flowers in her hand are from a Syrian ivory carving of a lady. The flowers are lotuses, as her name, Serpot, means "lotus." The woman behind Ashteshyt is carrying a false beard, helmet, and clothing of the enemy army for Ashteshyt's disguise. At the top of the posts are Assyrian-style sphinxes. In the canopies above are scenes of the queen hunting lions, a common scene for Assyrian kings.

**Pages 10 & 11:** The camp scene is based on three similar scenes of the camp of Ramses II at the battle of Kadesh. The camp is surrounded by a wall made of the soldiers' shields. In Egyptian art, Egyptian men have dark brown skin, women have yellow skin, and Assyrians have light skin. On the left of the camp scene is Ashteshyt's name in hieroglyphs.

**Page 12:** The queen and her sister greet each other. To either side of them are wall tapestries with Isis on the left and Osiris on the right, and their names in hieroglyphs. Below the god and goddess are scenes of the queen fighting Assyrian monsters. Above, in the canopy, the queen overpowers two winged bulls, and on either side a griffin and an ostrich fight. This design comes from an Assyrian cylinder seal found in 2001 on an excavation at Çadir Höyük in Turkey (in which the author was a participant). On top of the posts are griffins.

**Page 13:** Egyptian armies were usually accompanied by drums and trumpets. The trumpets gave signals to the troops loud enough to be heard over the sounds of fighting. The shapes of these two trumpets are inspired by the ones found in Tutankhamen's tomb.

**Page 14:** The queen is shaded by a parasol, as the king is portrayed in Assyrian art. She holds her bow turned away from her, which is a gesture of authority in both Egyptian and Assyrian art.

**Page 15:** The original papyrus specifically mentions that the Amazons had helmets with bulls' faces.

**Page 17:** The fleeing Egyptian with the bow is gesturing a sign of surrender.

**Page 19:** The hieroglyphs are the name of Pedikhons.

**Page 20:** Pedikhons's hairstyle is the "sidelock of youth" and indicates that he is a royal prince. He wears a heart-shaped amulet for protection on his chest, also typical of princes. Above in the canopy is a falcon, associated with the Egyptian gods Re and Horus. The falcon is holding symbols of eternity. Atop the posts are also falcons.

**Page 23:** The queen's armor is based on Assyrian examples. Above, in the canopy, Serpot visualizes her victory over Pedikhons, with him on bended knee begging for mercy. To the right the warrior goddess Astarte stands fully armed on top of a lion, giving her blessing to the queen. Her star symbol is overhead, in the center, with the sun on the left and the moon on the right. On either side they are faced by a row of defeated enemies. The posts are topped by griffin demons with the heads of eagles.

**Page 26:** To the left above Serpot is a vulture carrying a symbol for eternity; to the right above Pedikhons is a panther. Serpot's shield is decorated with the Assyrian sun symbol.

**Page 27:** To the left above Serpot is a lion; above Pedikhons is a falcon, carrying a symbol for eternity.

**Page 28:** This is an Assyrian version of the winged sun disk, a symbol borrowed from the Egyptians.

**Page 37:** Serpot and Pedikhons ride together in the same chariot, bows drawn, the reins wrapped around their waists. Running along beside them is Pedikhons's pet lion.

# FURTHER READING

Collier, Mark and Bill Manley. *How to Read Egyptian Hieroglyphs.* Berkeley and Los Angeles: University of California Press, 1998.

Davis-Kimball, Jeannine. *Warrior Women.* New York: Warner Books, 2002.

Hackett, General Sir John, ed. *Warfare in the Ancient World.* New York: Facts on File, 1989.

Healy, Mark. *Elite Series: New Kingdom, Egypt,* no. 40. London: Osprey Publishing, 1992.

Kitchen, K. A. "Excurcus G," in *The Third Intermediate Period in Egypt,* Warminster, England: Aris & Phillips, 1973, pp. 455–461.

Lichtheim, Miriam. *Ancient Egyptian Literature,* vol. 3, "The Late Period." Berkeley and Los Angeles: University of California Press, 1973.

Millard, Anne. *Going to War in Ancient Egypt.* Danbury, CT: Franklin Watts, 2001.

Salmonson, Jessica Amanda. *The Encyclopedia of Amazons.* St. Paul, MN: Paragon House, 1991.

Scott, Joseph, and Lenore Scott. *Egyptian Hieroglyphs.* New York: Hippocrene Books, 1998.

Spalinger, Anthony. "Psammetichus, King of Egypt," *Journal of the American Research Center in Egypt,* vol. 13. (1976): pp. 140–147.

Wilde, Lyn Webster. *On the Trail of the Women Warriors: The Amazons in Myth and History.* New York: St. Martin's Press, 1999.

Woods, Michael, and Mary Woods. *Ancient Warfare from Clubs to Catapults.* Minneapolis, MN: Runestone Press, 2000.

Zauzich, Karl-Theodor. *Hieroglyphs Without Mystery.* Austin: University of Texas Press, 1992.

Special thanks to my editor, Ginee Seo, and to:

James Allen
Anthony Askin
Diane Bergman
Mary Gow
Polly Kanevsky
Michael Nelson
Samuel Paley
Diana Craig Patch
James Romano
David Silverman
Virginia Skrelja
Josef Wegner

The hieroglyphic translations are by
Jennifer Houser Wegner, PhD,
Research Scientist, Egyptian Section,
University of Pennsylvania Museum of
Archaeology and Anthology.

Atheneum Books for Young Readers • An imprint of Simon & Schuster Children's Publishing Division • 1230 Avenue of the Americas • New York, New York 10020 • Copyright © 2005 by Tamara Bower • All rights reserved, including the right of reproduction in whole or in part in any form. • The text of this book is set in Cantoria. • The illustrations are rendered in watercolor and gouache on paper. • Manufactured in China • First Edition • 10 9 8 7 6 5 4 3 2 1 • Library of Congress Cataloging-in-Publication Data • Bower, Tamara. • How the Amazon queen fought the prince of Egypt / written and illustrated by Tamara Bower.—1st ed.•
p. cm. • Summary: Serpot, ruler of a land where women live free, without men, leads her Amazon warriors in battle against Prince Pedikhons of Egypt, who has come to see for himself if women can equal men, even in battle. Includes notes about Assyrian and Egyptian culture and hieroglyphics. • ISBN 0-689-84434-4 • [1. Amazons—Fiction. 2. Kings, queens, rulers, etc.—Fiction. 3. Princes—Fiction. 4. Sex role—Fiction. 5. Assyria—History—Fiction.] I. Title. • PZ7.B6756Ho 2005 • [Fic]—dc22   2004001781